Snowballs and Coconuts

by Cheryl Crouch

BEACON HILL PRESS
OF KANSAS CITY

Copyright 2007
by Beacon Hill Press of Kansas City

Printed in the United States of America

ISBN-13: 978-0-8341-2295-6
ISBN-10: 0-8341-2295-2

Cover Design: Kristina Phillips
Illustrator: Steve Bates

Editor: Donna Manning
Assistant Editor: Allison Southerland

Note: This story is based on the life of O. L. King (called Oscar in this book), an early missionary to Antigua. It is part of the *Kidz Passport to Missions* curriculum.

10 9 8 7 6 5 4 3 2 1

Contents

What More Could I Want?

Boom!

Ten-year-old Oscar smiled as he swung the heavy hatchet with all his might. He liked feeling his muscles work. He also liked watching his pile of wood kindling grow faster than his brother's pile.

Boom!

A chunk of wood flew past him.

"Watch it! You're going to put my eye out," his younger brother said.

"It's not my fault," Oscar answered. "You shouldn't work so close to me, Sam. Drag your wood over there." Oscar pointed to an area far away from the woodpile.

A tan hat covered Sam's wavy brown hair, and flaps hung down over his ears. Still, each of Sam's cheeks had a bright red spot on it. Oscar didn't know if the red came from the cold, or the hard work, or anger.

"That's not fair," Sam pouted. "Why should I have to drag my wood? You're heaps older than me. You take yours over there and chop it."

Oscar always had to do more. It wasn't his fault he was older. He said, "I won't. I got here first."

"Did not."

"Did too."

"Boys, you better quit fighting and get to work," said Ruth, their older sister. She strutted by, her long skirt swishing around her legs. "Mama said if you finish chopping the wood, you can pick wintergreen to flavor the candy." She stuck her nose in the air and announced, "*I'm* going to the mercantile [MER-kuhn-teel] with Mama."

"Lucky!" Sam declared. "Are you getting something special for Christmas?"

"Yes," said Ruth. "Mama says she's going to trade some of our butter and eggs for store-bought sugar. She wants it for her Christmas baking this year."

"Anything else?" Oscar asked.

Ruth hesitated. "Maybe. It depends on how much Mr. Watson gives us for our butter and eggs. Of course, if Mama gets anything for you, I'll have to keep it a secret."

Oscar grinned. "Too bad you're going with Mama. She can't get you any gifts."

"Maybe she already has my gifts," Ruth mumbled as she stomped away.

"Start dragging, Sam, so I can get back to work," Oscar said.

Sam put down his hatchet and crossed his arms. He tried to look tough.

"OK, fine!" Oscar wedged his tool into the heavy piece of wood and pulled it away from his brother. Then he pulled the hatchet free and started chopping again.

Oscar wanted plenty of wood to keep their room warm when they opened presents. And Mama would need wood to keep the stove hot to bake their Christmas lunch.

✳ ✳ ✳

"Do you think Mama will get us candy for Christmas?" Sam asked. He plucked shiny wintergreen

leaves from the small shrub they had discovered in the woods.

Oscar crushed a leaf and held it up to his nose. He breathed in deeply. "Why do you want candy from the store? There's nothing as good as the molasses candy we make, especially with the wintergreen flavor."

"I don't know. I think I like the hard, red candies we had last Christmas better than anything else." Sam stuffed a handful of leaves into his coat pocket. "Do you think we've got enough? My toes are frozen!"

Oscar did not want to leave. He loved the woods, especially in the winter. "Oh, all right," he answered. "Let's head back."

Sam led the way down the snow-covered path. "I'm glad Granny and Gramps are coming for Christmas this year," he said over his shoulder. "Ruth says they're rich. Is that true?"

"Not compared to Great-Aunt Jane. Compared to us, I guess they are," Oscar answered.

Sam stopped walking and turned to look at Oscar. He cocked his head to one side and asked, "Why don't we have money?"

"We don't need it," Oscar replied, pushing past Sam to take the lead. "We grow our own wheat and corn for bread. We grind our own cane for sugar. And we have animals for meat, milk, cheese, butter, and eggs. What more do we need?"

"I'm not talking about what you need," Sam tried to explain. "I'm talking about what you want. Isn't there anything you want?"

As the two brothers came out of the woods, Oscar caught sight of their log cabin tucked between two snow-covered hills. The soft light of a kerosene lamp flickered through the windows, and smoke rose in lazy curls from the chimney. He sniffed the crisp winter air and caught the scent of hickory from the smoke.

"No," Oscar answered. "I think I've got everything I want."

* * *

Mama and Ruth had returned from the tiny, country store in Green Valley.

"No peeking," Mama told the boys, as they stood by the door and stomped the snow from their boots. She and Ruth giggled as they tucked wrapped packages into cabinets.

Papa stoked the fire in the stove. "You did a good day's work, Boys. Tomorrow will be even busier," he said. "Your mama and sister will be stirring, mixing, baking . . ."

"And cleaning," Mama interrupted, now slicing potatoes for dinner.

Ruth groaned.

"A house on Christmas Eve is no place for a man," stated Papa.

"What will we do?" asked Oscar, taking a seat at the table.

"We must do our part and help prepare for the celebration of our Lord's birthday. First, we'll dress that wild turkey we caught. Then we better choose a Christmas tree."

"This year it's my turn to pick it!" Sam declared happily, leaning his elbows on the table.

"It is not," Oscar argued. "You chose last year. I remember we had a short, fat tree last year. You always choose short, fat trees."

"Uh-uh," Sam said, sticking out his lower lip.

"Uh-huh," Oscar insisted, crossing his arms.

"That's enough," Papa scolded. "Sam, I think Oscar is right. It's his turn to choose the tree. But that means it's your turn to put the star on top."

Sam stopped pouting. "Will Granny and Gramps and our uncles be here to watch me?" he asked.

Papa smiled. "They should be here," he answered. "And according to Granny's letter, they're bringing a surprise."

Oscar shivered with excitement. Christmas was his favorite day of the year. And he had a feeling this year would be the best Christmas ever.

※　※　※

Oscar snuggled down under his quilts. He stretched his legs until his feet touched the warm brick wrapped in soft cloth. Mama always placed one at the bottom of his bed. "Mmm," he murmured happily. All of a sudden, his brother's voice interrupted Oscar's sleepy thoughts.

"Papa," Sam called from the other side of the bed.

Oscar heard footsteps, and then Papa opened the door to their small room at the back of the cabin.

"Did someone call me?" he asked.

Sam answered, "Papa, do you ever want anything?"

Papa chuckled. "Sure, Son. Plenty of things. What do you have in mind?"

"Well," Sam continued, "are there things you would like to have, but you don't have the money to buy them?"

"Sometimes," Papa admitted. "Instead of thinking about what we don't have, we should be thankful for what God has given to us. If you had a nickel, Sam, what would you buy?"

"A whole nickel!" Sam exclaimed. "I'd buy the biggest jar of red candy I could find." He lay quiet for a moment, and then added, "Oscar said *he* has everything he wants."

Papa chuckled again and reached out to ruffle Oscar's hair. "I'm glad to hear that, Oscar. It's good to be content. But someday, there'll be something you want. That's not a bad thing. Just don't ever let that something come between you and God."

"All right, Papa," Oscar answered.

His father pulled the door shut, and Oscar lay in the darkness. He enjoyed the warmth of the quilts and the pleasant drowsiness that comes with a full belly. He could not imagine what more he could want.

But the very next day, he would find out what his papa meant.

2
Bread and Cheese

About 15 miles away from Oscar's home in Green Valley, a short, blond-headed boy named Ben lived outside the town of Littlefield. While Ben appeared stocky and strong, both the clothes he wore and the farm where he lived looked well-worn and untidy.

* * *

Ben loaded his sore arms with the wood he had chopped, carried it inside, and dumped it beside the stove.

"Thanks, Ben," his mama said, as she slid a loaf of bread into the oven. "Are you hungry?"

Ben nodded and pulled off his thin coat.

Mama smiled. "You're always hungry."

"Do you think Papa will be home . . . ?" Ben stopped short. He did not want to upset his mama.

"Maybe," she answered in a hopeful voice. "But probably not. He said there was another meeting at the old schoolhouse. The men want to talk about farming."

Ben felt his shoulders droop. He knew what that meant. His father was drinking and would not be in a happy mood when he came home. There would be no hugs, laughing, or teasing. Ben would pretend to be asleep, as usual.

"Are you going to read tonight?" Ben asked, trying to cheer up his mother.

"I shouldn't," Mama answered, shaking her head. "I need to clean this house so I can help you with the outside chores tomorrow." She looked at the dirty dishes and the floor that needed to be swept. Then she shrugged. "Maybe I will read—just until the bread is baked."

Ben ran to the shelf and reached behind the flour container. He pulled down a small, green book with fancy designs on the cover. It was their only book, and they kept it hidden. Ben knew his mama did not want Papa to destroy the book when he was upset.

Ben handed the book carefully to his mother.

"God bless Mrs. Moore for giving me this book and teaching me to read it." Mother gently turned the pages and found her bookmark. "Here we are," she said. Ben could tell by her voice she was feeling happier.

Although his mother stumbled over the words, Ben listened as she read:

These couchings and these lowly courtesies
Might fire the blood of ordinary men,
And turn pre-ordinance and first decree
Into the law of children.

"What does 'couchings' mean?" Ben asked.

Mother sighed. "I don't know, Ben. I told you Shakespeare lived a long time ago. He and Julius Caesar are famous. People talked differently in those days. Try to listen when I read and enjoy it."

Ben nodded. "I'm sorry, Mama. I'll be quiet." And he was—until the smell of bread filled the cabin. He was afraid his mother had forgotten the bread. What if it burned?

Ben clutched his growling stomach and imagined the agony of watching his mother start over. First, she would have to mix the yeast with a bit of warm water. Then she would add flour and knead—wait an eternity. Then she would punch the dough down, and wait again. Finally, she would form the loaf, and wait some more.

Ben could hardly stand the thought. But he did not want to interrupt his mother again. He swung his legs impatiently, and then he started tapping on the tabletop.

Mother continued to read:

O mighty Caesar! Dost thou lie so low?
Are all thy conquests, glories, triumphs, spoils,
Shrunk to this little measure?

Suddenly, Ben cried, "The bread!" He leaped from his chair. "It's burning!"

His mother quickly put her book on the table and jumped up. She pulled on her mitts and opened the oven door. "Silly boy. It's just now ready."

"Whew!" Ben was relieved when he saw the golden crust and smelled the heavenly scent.

"Put the book away," Mama said. "Tonight, we're going to celebrate. I don't know what we're celebrating, but we'll each have a slice of cheese with our bread."

❋   ❋   ❋

After dinner, Ben helped his mother with the chores. There were many chores to do, even though their farm was small. Then, as Ben washed his face and hands and got ready for bed, his mother surprised him.

"Ben, how would you like to go to Littlefield tomorrow?" she asked.

"Yes!" Ben shouted. In the glow of their lantern, he could see the excitement on his mother's face.

"Mrs. Patterson told me the stores are decorated for Christmas. And since tomorrow night is Christmas Eve, there'll be fireworks!"

"What are fireworks?" Ben asked.

* * *

Ben pulled his thin blanket up around him, but he could not go to sleep. He shivered with excitement as he thought about their trip to town. He closed his eyes and tried to picture bright, colorful fireworks exploding high in the night sky. Ben could hardly believe he would see them the next night. He had a feeling this could be the best Christmas ever.

3

Granny's Christmas Box

"I can't believe it happened again!" Oscar's father declared. "Three years in a row! I'm sure it was that fox."

Oscar stood beside his father and brother, staring in dismay at the empty turkey pen. He noticed signs indicating the bird had put up a good fight before the fox dragged it away.

"What will we have for Christmas? Can we butcher a hog like we did last year?" Sam asked, hoping his father would say yes.

Oscar perked up immediately. He remembered the tender spare ribs were delicious.

Papa shook his head. "Last year the fox stole our bird several days before Christmas. We don't have time to butcher a hog this year. It's Christmas Eve. If we get lucky, we'll get a couple of rabbits. Or we could try to catch a possum."

Oscar grimaced. He did not like greasy possum meat.

* * *

Oscar and his father each got a rabbit. They took them home for the "women" to prepare. Next, Oscar, Sam, and their father went to choose a tree.

Oscar took his responsibility of choosing a tree very seriously. He wanted a tree that would almost scrape the ceiling of their cabin, yet have just enough room for the star on top. The tree had to have a nice

18

overall shape too. Father said Christmas trees should point like arrows.

Oscar walked slowly around a tall fir, leaving boot prints in the snow. "This one is almost right," he declared. "But I don't like this branch." He tugged on the green needles and shook his head. "It sticks out too far."

"So cut it off!" Sam exclaimed. "Papa, make him stop! This is the 13th tree we've looked at. We'll miss Christmas!"

Papa cleared his throat. "This tree is as perfect as they come, Oscar. I'll cut that branch off myself. Let's start chopping."

❊   ❊   ❊

"They're here!" Sam yelled when they came within sight of the cabin. He dropped his rope and ran ahead.

Papa laughed and picked up the rope. "Do you want to go too?" he asked Oscar. "I can get the tree home from here."

"Sure! Thanks, Papa," he called, running after his brother.

Inside the cabin, Granny smothered Oscar and Sam with hugs and kisses. "You've both grown!" Granny told them. She sounded surprised.

Gramps, who had fought in the Civil War, stood up straight and gave Oscar a grand salute. "How is my eldest grandson?" he asked.

Oscar laughed and returned the salute. "I'm fine, Gramps. It's good to see you!"

His two uncles, who weren't much older than him, each punched him on the arm in a friendly greeting. He punched them back.

Johnny, the younger uncle, put him in a choke hold and rubbed the top of his head. Oscar wriggled free and wrestled Johnny to the floor. Matthew, the older uncle, piled on top of them.

Granny and Mama both called, "No wrestling in the house, Boys."

Just then, Papa swung the door open and stood looking down at them. Oscar and Johnny scrambled to their feet.

"You can roughhouse in the barn tomorrow," Papa said. "Right now I need help getting this tree in, Fellas."

* * *

Oscar sat and admired the decorated tree. He had never seen a prettier one, especially since Papa had trimmed the branch. The tree was so tall, Sam could barely get the star on top!

Papa sat beside the tree and opened the large family Bible. He began reading the Christmas story to the family.

Oscar had memorized the story from Luke chapter 2. His parents had said Jesus' birthday is the reason Christians celebrate Christmas. Still, he wondered, "Does Papa have to read the story now? Why can't he read it after we open Granny's Christmas box? Then I could concentrate on the story instead of wondering what's inside the box."

Oscar shifted his position on the floor in order to see the box better. He had watched Papa carry it in, and it looked heavy. He tried to guess what might be inside.

Papa closed the big Bible with a loud thud, and Oscar jumped.

"He's finished already?" Oscar thought.

"Granny, do you want to tell us about your box now?" Papa asked.

Granny nodded yes and smiled. When she had everyone's attention, she began. "As you know, my sister Jane and her husband Frank live in the city. Frank's business has done quite well."

Oscar wished Granny would just open the box. Everyone knew about her rich sister Jane, because Granny wrote about her in every letter.

Granny continued, "Jane knew Gramps and I were going to be with you for Christmas, and she sent me this box. She asked me to share the contents with you and wish you a merry Christmas."

Mama said, "Isn't that sweet," and all the adults nodded. Oscar, Ruth, Sam, Johnny, and Matthew began to crowd around the box.

Granny cleared her throat. "I will pass out whatever is in the box."

Oscar understood that meant Granny wanted their attention again. He and the other kids parted like the Red Sea, and Granny walked through the opening. She told them to sit on the floor.

"I'll need a hammer with a claw foot," Granny said.

Papa got the tool and helped Granny pry open the box.

She gasped as Papa lifted off the lid. Oscar could hardly wait to see what was inside!

4

Oranges, Chocolate, and Coconut

At last, Granny held up a bright orange ball about the size of an apple. "An orange!" she declared.

Oscar licked his lips. He had heard about oranges, but he had never tasted one.

He watched with fascination as Granny began to peel the orange covering off, revealing a smaller, white ball inside. He sniffed the air and grinned at Johnny and Matthew. If it tasted as good as it smelled, it would be a real treat!

Next, Granny showed them how to divide the orange into small sections. She pulled the sections apart and gave each person a slice.

Oscar felt a little unsure about tasting his piece. It felt soft and mushy between his fingers. He waited until Johnny and Matthew tasted their bites. They chewed and smiled and looked at Granny for more.

Oscar put the orange slice between his lips and bit down. A squirt of juice shot out and hit Matthew on the forehead. Matthew wiped his face and looked around, trying to figure out what hit him. Oscar giggled. The juice tasted wonderful, but the outside covering was thick. Oscar spit the seeds into his hand and finally swallowed the rest.

He leaned over to Sam and whispered, "I like it, but I think I'd just as soon have a Royal Beauty from the apple bin in the garden."

Sam nodded and whispered, "Me too."

Mama said, "Mmm. What a delicious fruit. Thank

you, Granny." She looked at the boys and Ruth and raised her eyebrows.

"Yes, Granny, thank you!" Ruth said right away.

The boys added, "Yes, thanks."

Granny paused, and then she reached into the box and pulled out a tin. "Chocolates!" she exclaimed.

"Oh!" Oscar said. This was another food he had only heard about.

"What's chocolate?" Sam whispered in his ear.

"Candy," Oscar answered.

Sam's eyes lit up, and he sat up straighter.

Granny pried the tin open and reached inside. She handed the first shiny, dark brown square of chocolate to Mama. Then she gave Gramps, Papa, and the kids each a piece. Finally, she took one out for herself.

Everyone held their piece of chocolate and waited. It reminded Oscar of Communion.

Oscar's chocolate started to melt in his hand. When Granny gave the OK to taste the chocolate, he did not hesitate. But as quickly as Oscar bit into it, he wanted to spit it out. It did not taste like peppermint or wintergreen or any of the flavors of candy he had ever tasted. Of course, he had to be polite, so he swallowed his bite.

"Sam, would you like the rest of mine?" Oscar asked.

Sam looked disappointed. He gazed at the rest of his own piece and shook his head. "It's nothing like the red candies from the store," he whispered.

Oscar knew he had to finish his piece. He took a deep breath, popped the chocolate in his mouth, chewed, and swallowed before he breathed again. "Thank you, Granny. I'll always remember you gave me my first taste of chocolate."

Granny beamed.

"There are more oranges and more chocolates for us to enjoy tomorrow," she said. "Now I want to show you the most curious thing of all. My sister wrote to me about it." Granny reached into the box and pulled out a dark brown object. It was larger than the oranges. It was almost round; and it had long, stiff hairs growing on it.

Oscar laughed with delight. There were three round circles on the end. They made a face with two wide-open eyes and a round, open mouth.

"What is it?" asked Oscar.

"It's called a coconut," Granny said. "It grows on a tall, skinny tree called a palm."

"It's the biggest nut I've ever seen!" Sam exclaimed.

"Jane warned me it would be a tough nut to crack. I'll need a saw," requested Granny.

Oscar looked at his brother and sister and shrugged. A saw to open a nut!

Papa got the saw, and everyone crowded around as he followed Granny's instructions. He put the coconut on Mama's big cutting board on the kitchen table. He held the nut with one hand; and with the other hand, he pulled the saw back and forth across the end.

"Stop!" Granny cried. "Now I'll pour out the milk."

"Milk from a nut?" Ruth questioned.

"It's coconut milk," Granny explained, pouring the milk in a tin cup. She passed the cup around, and each person took a sip.

Oscar made a face. "This is terrible," he thought.

Finally, Papa got the strange nut open. Granny told him to break it into pieces. Then she explained the white part of the coconut was called the meat. She showed everyone how to pry the soft, white meat away from the hard, brown shell.

Oscar did not want to taste the coconut. He had not enjoyed the orange or the chocolate. And since he did not like the coconut milk, he doubted he would like the meat. How disappointing!

"Tomorrow is Christmas," Oscar reminded himself. "Maybe my parents will have better surprises. Yet, maybe I should give Granny's one more try. Besides, I might not have another chance to taste a coconut."

Oscar took a small bite. "Mmmm!" he exclaimed out loud. The meat was more firm than an apple; and it tasted even sweeter. He chewed slowly, enjoying the new flavor. After he swallowed, he declared, "That's the best thing I've ever tasted!"

Gramps laughed with delight. "It's good, isn't it?" he agreed.

"Do you want the rest of yours?" Oscar asked Sam.

"I sure do!" Sam answered quickly.

Oscar took another tiny bite of his own piece. "What about you, Ruth? Do you want all of yours?"

"Yes!" Ruth answered. "It's delicious."

Oscar spent the rest of the evening trying to trade anything and everything for more coconut, but no one would trade. He kept his piece in his pocket and only took small bites, making it last as long as possible.

As he crawled into bed that night, Oscar decided he had never had a better Christmas. He decided something else too. Someday, he would find a way to eat all the coconut he wanted.

5

A Trip to Littlefield

Ben lay on his back, blinking his eyes open. He heard movement in the cabin. He closed his eyes and listened. He heard his mother's footsteps, the stove door opening, and the crackling of the fire. Then he sniffed the air.

Hotcakes!

Ben opened his eyes wide. He must have slept soundly. He had not heard his father come home last night. He stretched his arms above his head until they bumped the wall behind the bed. He felt along the wall until his hands found his pants. He jerked them and finally snapped them free from the peg. The pants fell across his face and Ben giggled happily. He pulled them down under the covers, wiggling and squirming until he got them on.

Ben swung his legs out from under the blanket and sat up. All of a sudden, he remembered the trip to town. He hoped Papa was in a good mood and would go with them. Ben longed for the times when his father talked with him and teased him.

Ben grabbed his shirt and rushed into the kitchen. He did not see his Papa. Mama stood at the stove, flipping hotcakes. Ben was about to burst with excitement, but he did not want to disturb his father in case he was asleep in the next room. "I didn't wake up at all last night," he whispered.

"And I hardly slept," Mama answered out loud. "I guess that meeting lasted all night, because your father never came home." She lifted four steaming hotcakes off the griddle and piled them on a platter that already held a small mound. Then she poured more batter into the sizzling black pan.

"Was this good or bad?" Ben wondered. Papa always came home.

He did not know what to think.

But then Mama smiled at Ben. "Do you still want to go to town?" she asked.

"Oh, yes!" Ben shouted.

Mama stood up straight and lifted her chin. "Then let's make a day of it. Get that shirt on and eat as many hotcakes as you can hold. I'll take some for lunch and supper too. You know we can't afford to eat at the restaurant."

Ben was happy to obey. He pulled his shirt on, sat down, and started eating.

"When you're finished eating, quickly do your chores," his mother instructed. "I want to leave before anything or anyone changes our plans."

* * *

"Ben, quit running ahead!" his mother called again.

"Sorry, Mama." Ben watched his mother as she hurried to catch up with him. Ben thought his mother looked beautiful. She had on the dress she wore every day, but she had piled her hair up under a blue hat.

"Who are you watching, Ben?" she asked.

"You, Mama," he answered. "I like your hat."

Mama laughed. "It's seen better days. I've had it since before I met your father."

"You never wear it," Ben said.

"That's because I'm usually doing chores, Ben. Women buy hats to wear at parties and socials. I can't remember the last time I got invited to one of those," she said.

"Well, I'm sure people in town have never seen a hat like yours!" Ben said proudly.

Mama laughed. "Ben, some ladies get a new hat every year. They would not think my hat is so special."

"Oh." Ben wished he could buy his mother a new hat every year.

After a while, Ben asked, "Mama, why is Christmas so important?"

"What do you mean?"

"Why do people decorate and have fireworks?"

"It's the time of year when everyone tries to think of others and give gifts as an expression of their love."

"I remember getting this coat for Christmas," Ben said with a smile.

Mama shook her head. "It's been two years ago, and you can barely button it now. You definitely need a bigger size."

* * *

Ben tried to remember what Littlefield was like. He and his mother had not been to town for a very long time, because Father always did the shopping—if he had money.

"There's a post office, right?" Ben asked.

"Yes, and I hear they've opened a third general store," Mama said. "Imagine! Why would any town need more than one store?"

Ben could not think of one reason.

"Oh!" Ben exclaimed suddenly. "I remember watching the train come into town one time."

"That's right. Littlefield has a railway station."

Ben skipped with joy. "Can we go see it? Please? Do you think a train will come today?"

Mama laughed. "Yes, I think it will. We can sit at the station for hours if that's what you want to do. This is our day to do as we please."

* * *

Ben's heart beat faster as they approached Main Street. He had not realized there would be so many people! He tried to smile at each person and say hello. Most of them smiled at him too.

Ben stopped outside the huge glass window of the first general store they saw. It was filled with Christmas decorations. There were holly branches with bright red berries, glass ornaments, and big candles. Mama looked and looked. Ben tugged her toward the door.

As they stepped inside, Ben saw a fragile-looking vase with roses painted on it, a wooden toy wagon, a harmonica, and many other treasures! Mama reminded him not to touch anything. He wanted to know if the wagon really rolled, but he obeyed and left it alone. He soon realized there were more exciting things waiting to be discovered on every shelf.

His mother seemed to be as happy as he felt. She called his attention to a looking glass, and he showed her a clock he liked. He was full of joy. "Christmas is definitely the best time of year!" Ben thought.

He did not realize how long they had been in the store until his stomach started to growl. Mama giggled and said, "It sounds like it's time for some of those hotcakes."

* * *

As they headed to the next store, a rowdy group of boys ran by, laughing and pelting each other with snowballs. Ben turned to watch them.

"Do you want to play for a while?" Mama asked.

"Could I?"

"Sure. I think it would be good for you," Mama answered.

"I'll go look around in Moore's Drugstore while you play. I don't want to be in the middle of a snow-ball fight. In a little while, you can find me inside."

"Thanks, Mama!" he yelled, running after the boys.

Ben rarely played with other kids, but he was not shy. He ran down the street yelling, "Wait for me! I want to play."

The boys stopped running and yelling. They turned and stared at Ben.

"Hello!" he called. "I'm Ben. How do you play?"

"How do you play?" the oldest boy repeated. He turned to the others. "He doesn't know how to have a snowball fight."

"What kind of kid doesn't know how to throw snowballs?" a tall, skinny boy asked.

The group of boys laughed. Ben laughed with them.

"You play like this," one boy said. He threw a snowball hard at Ben's face. Ben ducked, but the ball caught the top of his head. The boy cheered.

"Good aim, Ted!" the others yelled.

Ben smiled and said, "That didn't hurt."

The skinny boy bent over, formed a ball, and fired it at Ben. It hit his shoulder. Another boy threw a snowball and hit Ben's leg.

Ben quickly saw he would have to defend him-self. He bent down and started making snowballs. But there were at least seven boys, all aiming at him. He could not cover his head and make snowballs at the same time. He turned his back, only to find they had

31

formed a ring around him. They were throwing balls faster than he could make them. And every time he looked up, he got hit in the face. Finally, he kept his head down and just threw. The boys laughed wildly and yelled, "Missed again!"

Ben decided he'd had enough of the game. "All right!" he yelled between snowballs. "You win! I'm going to find my mama."

"You'll go to your mama when I say," the older boy commanded. The other boys laughed in a mean way.

For the first time, Ben felt afraid.

"Did you see his mother?" the skinny boy asked. "She's wearing an old ragged dress, and you should see her hat." The boys howled with laughter.

Ben flew into the skinny boy's stomach and began pounding the boy with both fists. It surprised and pleased Ben to hear the boy cry. He wanted to hurt the boy. "I'll teach you to talk about my mama!" he yelled.

Then Ben felt arms pulling him up. He thrashed and kicked. The boy named Ted turned Ben around and gave him a solid punch in the stomach. Ben bent over in pain. Ted followed with a swift upward punch to his face.

As Ben tried to regain his balance, he heard a boy yell, "Here comes a grown-up. Let's clear out!" Ben heard footsteps running away.

He blinked and looked around. The boys were gone.

"Are you all right?" a deep voice asked. A gentle arm steadied him.

Ben looked up into a stranger's kind eyes. "Yes, I . . . I think so." Then he covered his eyes and wept.

The nice man asked, "Do you live in town?"

Ben shook his head. "My mama and I came to look at the Christmas decorations," he explained.

"That's what I figured. Me too. Those town boys can be downright mean to country guys like us. Do you want me to help you find your mother? I'll tell her what happened."

Ben said, "Oh! No, Sir. Please don't do that. I don't want her to know. But thank you for your help."

❊ ❊ ❊

Ben and his mother saw a train come into Littlefield. They saw the stores lit up with beautiful Christmas decorations. And when it grew dark, Ben saw his first fireworks. He oohed and aahed along with his mother.

Although Ben saw many amazing things in Littlefield, he did not feel Christmas in his heart anymore.

6

A Difficult Decision

(Two Years Later)

Oscar pulled the mare up in front of Gramp and Granny's old country homestead just outside of Littlefield. He felt proud and relieved. He could not believe his parents had let him make the long trip alone.

The door of the house opened, and Gramps came out. He stood tall and saluted. "Hello, General," he called. "Where're you going?"

Oscar grinned. "Papa said I could come for Christmas!" he answered.

Gramps smiled and said, "Hitch your horse to the rail. We'll take care of him after you've warmed up a while."

* * *

While Granny cooked supper, Oscar sat with Gramps, Matthew, and Johnny in front of the big fireplace. The fire sputtered and crackled and gave out good heat.

Gramps handed Oscar a shiny winesap apple.

Oscar bit into it. "This is delicious!" he said. "It's so juicy."

Gramps nodded. "These are the best apples in the country. There's no better eating."

"I've only tasted one thing I like better," Oscar admitted.

Grandpa looked surprised. "And what's that?"

"The coconut from Granny's Christmas box."

"You mean the one we brought to your house two years ago? You still remember that?"

Oscar nodded. "I'll never forget it. Someday I'm going to have all the coconut I want to eat."

"How?" Matthew asked. "You may never see another one."

"I don't know yet," Oscar said. "I found a picture of one in a book at school. The book said coconuts grow in the tropics. I've told the other kids coconuts taste delicious, but they don't believe me. They don't think I've ever eaten one."

"Do they tease you?" Matthew asked.

"They call me coconut boy," Oscar admitted. "They say I'm going to turn into a coconut someday."

Matthew and Johnny laughed. "Coconut boy," Johnny repeated. "That's good."

"I saw a coconut in town once," Gramps said. "But I haven't tasted any since that Christmas at your house."

"Supper's ready," Granny called.

＊　＊　＊

"Oscar, would you like to go into Littlefield and see the Christmas sights?" asked Gramps. "I need to get some things."

"Yes, please!" Oscar answered.

"I'll give each of you boys a dime to spend in town," Gramps announced. He handed Oscar a shiny, silver coin.

Oscar stared at it. "Wow! A whole dime to spend on anything I want!" he exclaimed. He had never had so much money. He wondered, "Should I get a gift for Mama? Or something for Papa? What about Ruth and Sam? Maybe I'll find something for each of them."

* * *

Oscar enjoyed the two-mile walk to town. Johnny and Matthew kept him laughing most of the way. He kept his hand in his pocket, rubbing his dime as he walked.

He saw the lights long before they reached Littlefield. He had never seen such bright lights before.

"It's quite a sight, isn't it?" Gramps asked. "You should look in all the stores before you decide how to spend your money. There are three general stores and a drugstore."

Oscar could not imagine it. He thought the tiny mercantile at home was unbelievable.

When they reached town, Oscar looked at each decorated window before going into the store. He became more and more confused by all of the choices. Still, he thought he should follow Gramps' advice.

When Oscar looked through the large plate-glass window at the front of the grocery store, he gasped. He saw a coconut! One coconut!

A small sign beside it read: *Ten Cents.*

Oscar smiled and quickly grabbed the door knob. He had to get the coconut before someone else bought it.

As Oscar twisted the knob, he heard a voice inside him say, "Don't buy the coconut."

He looked through the window again and licked his lips, as he remembered its sweet taste. If he bought the coconut, he could take it to school and prove his claim.

"Don't buy the coconut," the voice said again.

His parents had taught him to obey that voice. They said sometimes that's how God talks to people.

Oscar wanted to obey God. But he had never faced a decision as hard as this one.

He wondered why he should not buy the coconut. There was nothing wrong with coconut. And Gramps had told him he could spend his dime however he wanted.

Oscar took one last look at the coconut, and then headed across the street to the drugstore. He stood outside, looking at the window display. He saw a small, red New Testament. The little sign beside it read: *Ten Cents.*

The voice inside Oscar said, "Buy the testament."

That did not make sense. Oscar had just received a Bible for his birthday. He did not need a testament. But Oscar felt certain he should buy the Bible. Oscar pushed open the door and went inside to the clerk.

"What can I get for you, Young Man?" he asked.

Oscar took a deep breath. "I guess I'll buy that red New Testament."

The clerk smiled and handed the book across the counter to Oscar. Oscar took it and flipped through the pages, but all he could think about was the sweet taste of coconut.

7

An Investment

Oscar reached into his pocket and slowly pulled out his dime. He held it in his hand a moment before giving it to the clerk.

"I think you've chosen the finest Christmas present there is," the clerk said.

Oscar tried to return his smile. "I hope so," he answered, then he headed out the door.

Oscar wanted to see the coconut one more time before he looked for Gramps. He headed across the street and *BAM!* He felt a cold blow to his left ear. He turned to see what had hit him. *BAM!* Another hit, right in the face!

He wiped the snow from his eyes and blinked. Standing across from him was a short, stocky boy who looked slightly younger than himself. The boy stood with his arm cocked, ready to throw another snowball. He looked angry.

In an instant, Oscar noticed the boy's blond hair sticking out through large holes in his hat. There were holes in the knees of his overalls too. And he was not wearing a coat, despite the snow on the ground.

"Do you want to have a snowball fight?" Oscar asked in a friendly voice.

The boy looked confused.

"I like throwing snowballs too," Oscar continued. "It's fun."

"Do you live in town?" the boy asked, stepping closer.

Oscar shook his head. "No, I live in the country. I came with my gramps and uncles to see the sights. My name is Oscar."

The boy dropped his snowball and smiled. "I'm from the country too." He wiped a hand on his dirty overalls and held it out. "My name's Ben."

Oscar shook Ben's hand. "So you came to see the Christmas decorations too?" he asked.

Ben shrugged. "I don't like Christmas, but Mama wants me to come with her and see everything."

"You don't like Christmas?" Oscar questioned. "Why don't you like Christmas?"

Ben looked down. "People aren't very nice at Christmastime," he answered.

"What about Jesus' birthday?" Oscar asked. "That's what Christmas is really about."

"Whose birthday?"

"Jesus."

"Who's Jesus?"

Oscar's eyes grew wide. He took a deep breath and said, "Jesus is God's Son." Oscar paused, thinking the boy would say, *"Oh! That Jesus."* But when the boy did not say anything, Oscar added, "Angels sang about Jesus' birth and told some shepherds who were in the fields watching their sheep."

The boy looked interested.

"And kings came from far away to see Jesus."

"Really?" the boy said. "There were angels and kings?"

Oscar put his hands on his hips and asked, "Doesn't your Papa read the Christmas story to you?"

Ben shook his head. "My papa can't read," he said softly. "But my mama is a good reader."

"Give him the testament," a voice said to Oscar. Oscar jumped. He had forgotten! He reached inside

his pocket and pulled out the little, red book.

"Would you like this?" Oscar asked the boy. "It tells about Jesus' birth, the shepherds, and the angels and kings! And it tells how Jesus grew up and made blind people see and crippled people walk."

Ben looked confused. "Do you mean I can have the book to keep?"

Oscar smiled and nodded, holding it out toward Ben. "Yes. For keeps. Your mama can read it to you."

Ben slowly reached out his dirty hand and took the book. "I guess some people are nice, after all," he said with a slight grin. He opened the book carefully and turned a few pages. Then he closed it and put it in his pocket. "Thank you, Oscar. I'm sorry I hit you with the snowballs. I thought you were one of those boys in the town gang." Ben patted his pocket and waved good-bye. "I can't wait to show Mama what you gave me!"

Oscar smiled. He felt happy. Now he understood why God wanted him to buy the New Testament instead of the coconut. He did not need to look at the coconut now. Instead, he went to find Gramps. Together they found his uncles and headed down the country road toward home.

"Oscar, what did you get with your dime?" Matthew asked.

Oscar replied, "What did you get with yours?"

"I got three sticks of candy and this ball," Matthew answered, pulling a small, red ball out of his pocket. "I already ate my candy."

"That looks like a fine ball," Gramps said.

"I got five peppermints and two marbles," Johnny said. "And I only ate one of my peppermints. I'm going to eat one a day, so they'll last almost a week."

They walked in silence for a while, and Oscar listened to the soft crunch of snow under their boots. Then Matthew said, "Hey, Oscar, you never told us what you bought."

"That's right," Johnny said. "Let's see it."

Oscar buried his hands deep in his pockets. "I'm not telling," he said. "It's a secret."

"A secret!" Johnny exclaimed, frustrated that Oscar would not tell. "That's no fun. Come on, you can trust your secret with us."

Oscar shook his head. "No. I'm not telling."

"I know," Matthew said, jabbing Oscar with his elbow. "You lost your dime, didn't you? And you're too embarrassed to tell."

"I didn't lose it," Oscar said. "I spent it on something nice. I just don't want to talk about it, that's all."

"All right, boys," Gramps said. "If Oscar doesn't want to tell, he doesn't have to."

The boys tramped along in silence for a while. But before the night was over, Oscar's uncles teased him about losing his dime.

Oscar knew his dime was not lost. He thought of it as an investment in a young boy's life. He often wondered if Ben made it home with the Bible. He hoped so, and he hoped the boy's mother read it to him.

8

Ben and Oscar

(Five Years Later)

Oscar practiced his sermon as he rode his new pony down the old country road. "It is by faith we are saved!" he bellowed. He leaned forward in the saddle and patted his pony's mane. "You got that, Bessie?"

Oscar could hardly believe the circuit preacher had asked him—a teenager—to fill in. But he insisted Oscar could fill his many pulpits while he was on a trip. Oscar did want to preach someday.

So Oscar began his journey with a hand-drawn map, a list of names, a bedroll, and his Bible. He spent a day or two at each location, preaching to people who did not have a full-time pastor in their community. He was surprised people listened to him, but they did. The more places he preached, the more excited Oscar became about doing God's work.

"Whoa!" he called, pulling up on the pony's reins. "I think we're at our next stop, Bessie."

The little building did not look like much. Oscar dismounted and tied Bessie to a tree, so he could look around.

The door stood partway open, and Oscar stepped inside the single room. "It doesn't look like a church," he mumbled. The floor was covered with tobacco juice, and he noticed holes in the walls. He ran his hand over one near the door. "A bullet hole!" he exclaimed. He looked up to find more of the same in the ceiling.

He went back out to get his Bible. "I'd better start

praying, Bessie," Oscar told his pony. "It looks like I might have a tough crowd tonight!"

* * *

"If you have a Bible with you tonight, hold it up," Oscar said, standing in front of about 20 men and a few women. They looked as rugged as the building.

A few people on the front row held their Bibles above their heads. But it was something about half-way back that caught Oscar's eye.

A stocky teenage boy with blond hair held a small, red New Testament above his head.

A voice inside Oscar said, "That's what you got for the price of a coconut."

* * *

After the service, Oscar shook hands and talked with those who had come. People lit their lanterns to prepare for the walk home. At last, Oscar made his way back to the boy with blond hair. It had to be Ben.

"Where did you get your New Testament?" Oscar asked.

The boy smiled. "How much time do you have? It's a long story."

Oscar sat down on the nearest bench and said, "I'm in no hurry."

The boy held the little book up as he said, "I wouldn't trade this book for any farm in the country."

"Why is that?" Oscar asked.

"Years ago, one Christmas Eve, a boy came out of the drugstore in Littlefield and gave me this New Testament. He told me the story of Christmas. I had never heard it before. Mama and I didn't get home that night until almost midnight. But Mama was so excited about the book, she stayed up all night reading by lamplight. When my papa came home, she kept reading. She spent most of Christmas Day reading it out loud to both of us. She read to us every evening.

"One night as Mama was reading the testament, Papa started crying. I'd never seen him cry. He dropped down on his knees and started talking to Someone I couldn't see. I didn't know why he was crying or who he was talking to.

"The next thing I knew, Papa jumped up and started clapping. He grabbed Mama and kissed her, and he kissed me. And then he took this little book and kissed it. He had an expression on his face I'd never seen before.

"A few days later, while Mama sat reading, her eyes filled with tears. She knelt down and talked to that same Someone I couldn't see. Then her face lit up and she said, 'Blessed Jesus!' She kissed the book too.

"Our home became a happy place. Neighbors started coming in to hear Mama read the Book. She and Papa prayed with them. After a while, there were too many people to fit in our little house. Papa thought of this place. It was an abandoned schoolhouse where all the men came to drink and gamble."

Oscar nodded and looked around. Now he knew why there were bullet holes everywhere.

"We plugged up most of the holes to keep out the wind, and now we use the building for our church," the boy said. "These things have happened because of this little book."

"Do you think you would recognize the boy who gave the book to you?" Oscar asked.

"No," the boy said. "We were just kids."

Oscar chuckled and asked again, "Are you sure

you wouldn't recognize him?" Oscar whistled and looked around.

Ben stared at Oscar. "It was you!" he shouted.

Oscar nodded and laughed.

Ben pulled Oscar to the front of the room and stood by him at the altar. "Look!" he shouted. "This is the boy who gave us the Bible!"

The men and women rushed to the altar. They hugged Oscar and pinched his cheeks and shook his shoulders until he thought he would surely be black-and-blue.

When everyone left, Ben invited Oscar home to meet his mother. On the way, Ben said, "Papa went to heaven a few years ago." "He shouted 'Glory' just before he died."

✳ ✳ ✳

The hugging started again as soon as Ben introduced Oscar to his mother. "You changed our lives forever, Young Man," she said.

Ben pointed to a chair.

Oscar sat down and said, "I remember I almost bought a coconut with my 10 cents, but God told me to buy the New Testament instead. I could almost taste that coconut!"

"I'm glad you obeyed God," Ben said, sitting in a chair across from Oscar. "Your 10 cents has brought many good things to my family and our neighbors. Our home changed completely, and Papa is in heaven with Jesus. Instead of a building where people gamble and drink, we have a church where people learn about God."

✳ ✳ ✳

Oscar spent the night in Ben's log cabin. The

boys talked and laughed together until the early morning hours.

The next morning was Sunday. People came from all around to meet the boy who had given them the New Testament and to hear him preach. Even though Oscar had not slept much, he preached a good sermon.

Before he mounted his pony to ride away, he hugged Ben and his mama one last time. "I don't know if I'll see you again," he said.

"Oh, you'll see us again," Ben answered. "If not on earth, we'll meet in heaven someday."

* * *

As it turned out, the boys did not have to wait long to see each other again.

9

Sweet Rewards

(Four Years Later)

Oscar watched the group of Bible college students walk by, laughing and talking. None of them glanced his way. He moved up farther under a big oak tree, hoping to hide in its shade.

Everyone at his new school seemed to have a friend, except for him. He felt out of place, because most of the other students were younger. Oscar had spent several years working to save enough money for college.

Oscar felt a bit afraid about being so far from home. He had traveled over 200 miles on a train to get to the school. The journey had been an exciting adventure, but he already missed his family—and it was only his first day. He wished he could see a familiar face.

Oscar smiled and reminded himself why he had come. He knew God wanted him to preach. Many people had told him this school was the best place to receive his training. Of course, it would be more fun if he had a friend. But he would study hard and learn all he could while he was here.

He strolled out from under the tree and headed to the dorms. "I might as well get settled," he thought. As he opened the door, someone rushed out of the building, almost bumping into him. Oscar jumped out of the way.

"I'm sorry," the young man said. "I need to pay attention to . . . Oscar?" he asked.

Oscar could not believe it. "Ben?" Oscar's face lit

up. "The first time we met, you pelted me with snow-balls. And now you're trying to knock me down!"

Ben laughed and pumped Oscar's hand. "I'm going to be a preacher!" Ben declared.

"You mean you're a student here? Of all the Bible colleges in the country, are you really enrolled at this one?" Oscar asked.

Ben nodded. "Yes. People told me it was the best. I'm feeling kind of lost, though. There's been a mix-up on the rooms. I got assigned to one that's full."

"Let's go see the dean," Oscar said with an even bigger grin. "That's no mix-up. I don't have a room-mate. How would you like to stay with me?"

✳   ✳   ✳

Two years later, Ben stood in front of Oscar in the long line of students wearing black graduation gowns. He turned around to look at his friend, and reached up to straighten Oscar's black graduation cap.

"Thanks," Oscar whispered. He tugged on the colored cords around Ben's neck. They showed Ben was graduating with top honors. "Congratulations on earning these."

Ben blushed. "Aw, it's no big deal," he said in a soft voice.

"I don't have any cords," Oscar pointed out.

"Well, I wouldn't have them, or this either," Ben said, pointing to his cap, "if you hadn't given me that New Testament."

The line moved forward and each boy took a few steps.

Oscar poked Ben in the back and said, "I'm glad I gave it to you. Your friendship these two years has been sweeter than that coconut. I'll miss you. China is a long way from here."

Ben nodded and turned back toward Oscar. His blue eyes clouded a bit. "I can't wait to tell the Chinese people about Jesus. I know you'll pray for me."

"I will," Oscar promised. He thought, "How many people from China will become Christians, all from the price of a coconut?"

"And I know you'll pray for me," Oscar added.

"Yes. Antigua is a long way from here too," Ben answered. "You're going to make a wonderful missionary."

The dean called, "David Jackson," and a tall, red-headed boy walked across the stage and received his diploma. Ben and Oscar got quiet and stood up straighter. They would be next.

✳ ✳ ✳

Oscar better understood how far away Antigua was after days and days on a large boat. He often read the letters Mama, Papa, Ruth, and Sam had sent with him. They encouraged him to listen to God's voice.

Oscar had been happy to see land again, but his trip was far from over. He met a guide, and they continued the journey on horseback.

Finally, the guide's dark face lit up with a smile. "Ah! Now we're getting close to your new home."

He led their horses onto a side road.

Soon, Oscar saw only tall, thin trees lining both sides of the dirt path. Each tree had long green branches growing out of the very top. The rows of trees stretched as far as he could see. "What is this?" he asked.

His guide turned to him in surprise. "They didn't tell you?" he asked.

"Tell me what?"

"Your mission home is in the middle of a 40-acre coconut grove." He smiled at Oscar. "Around here we eat coconut syrup on our hotcakes, coconut rice, coconut and breadfruit, and coconut with salt fish. For a snack, we have coconut candy. Or, there's always just plain coconut."

Oscar felt his mouth drop open. He remembered a promise he had made to himself when he was a young boy. Then he remembered the coconut he wanted to buy. He had chosen to obey God. Now God had called Oscar to serve Him in the middle of a coconut grove! "God is good," said Oscar.

"Yes, Sir," his guide said. "I sure hope you like coconut. Because that's one thing I can promise you. Around here, you'll get all the coconut you want."